I0648220

Elizabeth J. Hereford

Rebel Rhymes

and other poems

Elizabeth J. Hereford

Rebel Rhymes
and other poems

ISBN/EAN: 9783337272555

Printed in Europe, USA, Canada, Australia, Japan

Cover: Foto ©Andreas Hilbeck / pixelio.de

More available books at **www.hansebooks.com**

Rebel Rhymes

AND

OTHER POEMS

BY

ELIZABETH J. HEREFORD

———

NEW YORK AND LONDON

G. P. PUTNAM'S SONS

The Knickerbocker Press

1888

DEDICATED

TO

THE ARMY OF NORTHERN VIRGINIA.

·" Nor can there fail to arise the image of that other Army that was the adversary of the ' Army of the Potomac,'—and which, who can ever forget that once looked upon it ?—that array of ' tattered uniforms, and bright muskets '—that body of incomparable infantry, the ' Army of Northern Virginia', which for four years carried the Revolt on its bayonets, opposing a constant front to the mighty concentration of power brought against it ; which, receiving terrible blows, did not fail to give the like ; and which, vital in all its parts, died only with its annihilation." — Swinton's " Army of the Potomac."

CONTENTS

THE LAND OF DIXIE.

Where centuries with a ceaseless tide
Sweep o'er the nations that have died,
The nations that their course have run,
There lies a mighty fallen one.
In all her vestal robes pure white,
She perished in a single night,—
With prayers and tears and many a sigh,
Her lovers saw her fall and die
Upon the breast of Dixie.

They said, Alas ! we might have seen
Our lady fair a beauteous queen ;
While e'en the foe with bated breath,
Looked down upon her glorious death.
Alas ! Alas ! then let her rest,
With laurel on her brow and breast,—
Enshrined let all her glories lie
Beneath the ever radiant sky
That spans the land of Dixie.

The blood flowed, as the red, red wine
Flows from the clusters of the vine,
In waves about her peerless feet,
Pressed out of lives that held it sweet
To perish, that 't was half divine
To sleep in death 'neath freedom's shrine ;
They slumber on her tender breast,
The truest, fondest, bravest, best,—
The gallant sons of Dixie.

Our dead, how dear, with eyes tear-wet,
The living think upon them yet,—
How sacred the memorial fires,
That love in human hearts inspires ;
They 'll burn with ever radiant ray,
As long as darkness follows day.
And immortelles their bloom shall shed,
O'er marble couch, or grass-grown bed,
That holds the dead of Dixie.

O wind ! that mingles with the roar,
Of waters by the wave-kissed shore,
Or, like a blessing, breathes around
Our homes with sweet caressing sound,
Thou bringest now upon thy breast

No note of war, no dirge of death,
But seemest to whisper o'er and o'er,
Come quickly, O glad days of yore,
To all the land of Dixie !

The bitter dregs are drained at last,
The darkness dieth down the past.
Thy trials all with triumphs crowned,
Thy noble sons by toil embrowned,
Have made of every battle-plain,
A golden field of waving grain ;
Thy portals now are decked with flowers
And peace, and plenty in thy bowers,
O peerless land of Dixie !

THE OLD PLANTATION.

Runs a dark and restless river,
Seaward by a low batture,
On its breast the moonbeams quiver,
As in days of long ago.

There the old plantation lies
All dismantled and forlorn,
And the air is full of sighs
For the days of long ago.

O, the waving wealth of canes,
Bending with their emerald hues,
Footsteps down the long green lanes,
In the days of long ago.

Sounds of engines, far and near,
Grinding out the juices sweet,
Called like voices, loud and clear,
In the days of long ago.

4

Happy slaves their burdens bore,
Toiling, yet with cheerful faces,
Singing weird songs o'er and o'er,
In the days of long ago.

In the homestead, not a care ;
Sounds of love, and sounds of laughter ;
Orange blossoms, budding there,
In the days of long ago.

In the hush of all this gladness
Came the sound of martial drums,
And the land was full of sadness,
In the days of long ago.

Bridal blossoms all are dead,
Lanes all grass-grown, fields all yellow,
And the laughter, too, has fled,
With the days of long ago.

Still the rushing, restless river
Runs along the low batture,
All unchanged, it murmurs ever,
As in days of long ago.

A TEXAS IDYL.

From the far-famed Persian looms,
From the distant eastern lands,
Come the wondrous fabrics woven
By the toil of skilful hands ;
But upon the prairies brown,
Now is spread a robe more rare,
Wealth of blossoms, wealth of bloom,
Wealth of fragrance everywhere.

Brush of painter, poet's pen,
Strive in vain, they cannot reach
Nature's heights, their efforts grand,
Lifeless lie along the beach.
Like a blessing sweet as prayer,
On the prairie vast and wide,
Like a tender touch of heaven,
Falls the spell of eventide.

Rests upon the rough-hewn home,
Centred in a picture grand,

6

At the threshold, by the door,
Clustering now the children stand,
In the cooling evening hours.
Father smokes his pipe, at rest,
Mother, now the work is done,
Rocks the baby on her breast.

What tho' mighty monarchs die,
What tho' kingdoms great shall cease,
Here they know not crowns or care,
All is sweet content and peace.
Far away great cities rise
Mid the busy world of strife,
But no murmur of the tide
Mingles with their quiet life.

From the distance comes the song
Of the cowboy, wild and quaint,
Notes in numbers loud and strong ;
Now they quiver, now they faint,
Dying in a cadence sad,
Where the restless tramping feet
Of the mighty, moving herd
Crush the flowers frail and sweet.

O'er the nectar-ladened blooms,
Bearing burdens to and fro,
Float the busy little bees,
Softly humming as they go ;
Parting gleams of glory lie
On the hills far off and dim ;
The sunset clouds the picture frames,
And sets it in a golden rim.

O dream of beauty, fade not yet ;
One moment more,—alas ! it flies ;
The shadows come, like giants grim,
And bear it from my pleading eyes.
The darkness, in a mighty wave,
Flows down and hides the picture bright ;
In vain, my heart cries out, " Return ! "
It glides away into the night.

THE REBEL'S SWORD.

'T is the blade of a rebel
   Who sleeps 'neath the sod,
The sword of a soldier
   Now gone to his God.

Take it down gently,
   Touch it with care,
Blade of Toledo !
   No gems rich and rare

Can buy thee away,
   From thy place on the wall ;
For when the day darkens,
   And long shadows fall,

I gaze on thee sadly,
   And think of the day
When from the red field
   They bore him away,

And laid him so tenderly
  'Neath the green tree—
Our valiant young soldier,
  Who died to be free.

Then they took the sword sadly
  From out his cold clasp ;
Sadly, and solemnly,
  From out his death grasp.

And while wiping away
  Each dark bloody stain,
We wept that he never
  Could wield it again.

Then take it down silently,
  The sword of my love ;
Breathe gently a prayer
  For the soul gone above.

For the soul of the rebel
  Who lies 'neath the sod ;
The soul of the soldier
  Now gone to his God.

SELIM.

A STORY OF FRONTIER LIFE.

Through a frontier forest brown.
Rides a slender maiden down
To the stream that like a thread
Of silver o'er its rocky bed
Unwinds itself 'mid briar and brake.
Down to the bosom of the lake,
Rides amid the sunset's gold,
That about her seems to fold ;
And her cheeks, are all aglow,
Sounds her singing soft and low,—
Like sweet-toned Eolian notes
Through the evening air it floats,
Though 't is but a time-worn hymn
Sounding down the vistas dim.

'Mid the whisperings of the breeze
Through the low-branched waving trees,

Comes a wild, blood-curdling cry.
Hark, how the echoes wake and die,
They come e'en now, the savage foes,
Like the swift arrows from their bows.
Riding down the tangled way
Of the forest, wild dismay
Holds the maiden breathless there,
Breathless with her heart's despair ;
The fearful cries ring out again,
And then she gives her horse the rein.
So fast they fly, the shadows seem
Like dancing demons by the stream.

O noble steed, of noble sire,
Not faster does the leaping fire
Sweep o'er the bosom of the plain,
Or breath of tempest o'er the main.
'T is well thou runneth like the wind,
For shadowy death runs fast behind.
There lies the cabin home, at last,—
The foeman, too, are coming fast,
Adown the shorter way they ride,
Through briar, and brake, by mountain side,
Speed on, or soon the poisoned dart
Will pierce thy fiercely-beating heart ;

For death, and torture, and untold woes,
Like demons ride with those bended bows.

They near the fence, that rail on rail
Lies serpent-like across the trail,
One moment, then he spurns the ground,
And clears it with one gallant bound !
Like lightning through the open door,
He rushes in—a moment more
The bar descends, without arise
The baffled rage of savage cries.
Down from her seat the maiden glides,
And stands by Selim's reeking sides ;
She draws his head close to her breast,
Her prayerful lips upon it pressed,
And hears afar the savage wail,
As darkness falls upon the vale.

Years of sorrow and joy have fled,
The years that go with noiseless tread,
The maiden is a matron grown,
The forests are fields, with seeds o'ersown ;
No more is heard the wild bees' hum,
No more the swallows go and come
About the rough-hewn cabin walls.

But morning breaks, and twilight falls
Upon a home, where pattering feet
Keep rythmic time to laughter sweet.
Oft by the doorway, in the sun,
Old Selim stands, his work is done ;
There you may see him, day by day,
Lazily dreaming the hours away.

CORRESPONDENCE.

This earth is but the mirror
  Of the glorious world above,
The land of the hereafter,
  The land of life, and love.
The sun that gilds the day
  With its life-awakening light,
The gentle moon that crowns the sky,
  And rules the realms of night ;
Fixed stars that drink the sunlight,
  And the wandering stars that burn
High in the arch of heaven,
  Each red comet in its turn ;
The fleecy clouds that skim the sky,
  Or dark, storm-ladened come ;
The zephyr with its gentle breath,
  The whirlwind's thrilling tone ;
The ocean in its fury,
  And the streamlet, breathing mirth ;

15

Trees with their moving banners green,
　　Each humble flower of earth ;—
All speak in heavenly language
　　Some soul-felt mystery
Of the home that is prepared us,
　　In the great eternity.
If man will take these lessons
　　To his weary world-worn heart,
They 'll lead him from the thorny paths
　　To seek that better part
Which leadeth through the darkness,
　　Up to a world of light,
Leaving earthly cares and sorrows
　　Buried in this world of night.

OUR SOLDIER.

Down the blossom-bordered lanes,
Through the rows of emerald canes,
    Our soldier went one day ;
All his heart with rapture glowing,
Dreams of glory round him flowing,
    Thus he rode away.

He sleeps beside a tranquil lake,
No sounds of strife his slumbers break,
    No tears for him are shed ;
But gentle winds above him toss
The tangled tendrils of the moss,
    Gray banners o'er his head.

While murmurous music seems to flow
From where the rustling rushes grow,
    And lotus flowers nod
    ir white heads on the summer air,
Sweet silent sentinels so fair,
    About the sacred sod.

He sleeps, and never through the canes,
Through the blossom-bordered lanes,
    Will he come again ;
Still is the heart within his breast—
O gallant soldier, take thy rest,
    Thy honor bears no stain.

FATHER RYAN.

IN MEMORIAM.

The New South, with her haughty tread,
  And fair, uplifted face,
Walks o'er the ashes of the dead,
  Leading the newborn race.

They hear no sounds of anguish rise
  Where Dixie's loving daughters
Once sang their sorrows 'neath the skies,
  By dark Babylonian waters.

How dim and indistinct they seem,
  The war ways 'neath the clouds,
The shifting shadows of a dream,
  Our heroes in their shrouds.

O proud young race ! the Old South cries,
  Look backward, where he sleeps,—
Her poet-priest, in death he lies ;
  Behold her, how she weeps !

What hand the silent lyre shall wake,
  To ring her martial measures ?
Who from the buried past now take
  The lost Pompeian treasures ?

What minstrel sing her lofty lays,
  And tell the wondrous story ?
Who now the conquered banner raise
  Unto the heights of glory ?

Rest, sunlit shafts, in holy light,
  About the sacred tomb ;
O softening shadows of the night,
  Fall lightly in the gloom !

For he who lies beneath the sod,
  Loved, with a proud devotion,
His country well,—next to his God.
  His be the patriot's portion.

Farewell, sweet singer, may thy bold
  Strains rise with the immortals,
Thy footsteps tread the paths of gold
  That lead from heavenly portals.

And all the yesterdays so sad,
  The yesterdays of sorrow,
Be lost forever in the glad
  Eternities of morrow !

LOUISIANA.

WRITTEN ON HER FREEDOM FROM RADICAL RULE.

From where the broad Pacific
Beats at the golden gates,
To where the wild Atlantic sweeps,
Storm-crowned, around the States,
There is no land divinely fair
Or beauteous as thou art ;
Enshrined like some rare jewel,
In every Southern heart.

Thou wert like some dead beauty,
With sweet flowers on thy breast,
And the crescent crown upon thy brow
Was dim with thy unrest.
There was a sound of wailing,
And her sister States all said :
The Queen, enchained and desolate,
Down-trodden, she is dead.

21

But the warm, resistless gulf-waves
Flowed up with measured beat,
And brought the quick life-pulses
Unto her pulseless feet ;
While the mocking-birds kept calling
From out her orange groves :
How could she die, and break the hearts
Of all her ardent loves ?

See, see ! she moves her chainéd hands,
A hush is on the sea—
Her fetters fall from out the land—
Goes up a cry, " She 's free ! "
How freshly bloom her gardens now,
On highland and on plain ;
Exultant her great river rolls
Amid her fields of cane.

A shout goes up from every hearth,
Where sorrow sat before,
And echoes back from strand to strand :
" Free ! free for evermore ! "
Her children from the " Lone Star State
Cry to her sons : " Well done !
How nobly you have worn your chains,
How bravely you have won ! "

Shine, Crescent, shine to all the earth !
Across the waiting sea,
Come ships, and bear her treasures forth,
Bring her prosperity.
Her people now with willing hands
Will welcome honest toil ;
And poverty and want shall dwell
No more upon her soil.

THE SCOURGE.

Where, barbed with tropic fires,
Are the arrows of the day,
And the stars, like gleaming lances,
Shine adown the sky's highway,—
Where the breezes, 'mid the blossoms
Of the orange and the lime,
Are breathing, odor ladened,
In a sultry, sunlit clime,—

Where the lagoons through the marshes,
Like serpents sinuous go,
'Neath trees, whose old gray branches
Wave sombre signs of woe,
And the mists creep up at morning,
Then from the broad day's frown
Flee back, to come at twilight,
Ghostlike, gliding swiftly down,—

There Death rises from the waters,
And with feet upon the strand,

Turns towards a sunlit city,
With cold eyes and beckoning hand.
Then the old prophetic warning
Is heard once more : " Behold,
One of the two together
Shall be taken from the fold."

The idol of the household
Drops its playthings at the door,
And turns its trembling footsteps
To the unseen, silent shore.
The bride in her fair beauty,
With the lovelight in her eyes,
Looks back to earth with longing
From the threshold of the skies.

The old, the young, the happy,
The worn with worldly cares,
The sowers of the golden wheat,
The sowers of the tares,—
Rise up and go forth quickly
Unto that beckoning hand—
Unto the feet of solemn death,
Unto the spirit land.

And homes are full of mourning ;
Fond eyes o'erflow with tears,
Eyes that will e'er be turning
To the realms of boundless years.
But voices from the darkness
Are calling : " Loved ones, come,
Through the valley of transition,
We will lead you gently home."

Now upon the earth-strewn coffins
Of the lowly and the lost,—
By the cold wild winds of autumn
The withered leaves are tossed.
But gentle spring returning
Will clothe them all with green,
Teaching nature's living lessons
Of the things that are unseen.

OUR CHIEFTAIN.

They say thou art forgotten,
  Chief of the great Southland ;
That thy people's vows are naught
  But ropes of frail sea sand.

Or, like the web the spider weaves
  In one short summer day,
Blown here and there by passing winds,
  And swept by storms away.

Believe it not,—our hearts are true ;
  Thy name can never die
While yet one flower drinks the dew
  Beneath the Southern sky.

Forget thee, never ! while one ray
  Of sunlight from the blue,
Falls earthward on the graves where lie
  Our soldiers, brave and true.

Ah ! in the dim hours of the day,
　　The silence of the night,
We seem to see the troops in gray
　　Sweep down from off the heights.

And shadowy forms by riverside,
　　And on fierce battle plain ;
Once more our gallant soldiers ride,
　　Our vessels speed the main.

Our bugle notes sound once again
　　Adown the valleys wide ;
The beat of drum, the clash of steel
　　We hear on every side.

Alas ! the conquered banner
　　Waves but in fitful dreams ;
Our armies grand are phantoms,
　　That ford the flowing streams.

Still, we with souls undaunted
　　Will sing our martial lays,
And tell to coming ages
　　The glory of those days.

And all about the sepulchres,
　　The graves of our defeat,

Will Poesy the pathways tread,
    And gather garlands sweet.

Garlands that ne'er shall wither,
    Of names that cannot die
While yet one flower drinks the dew
    Beneath the Southern sky.

Then, Chieftain of the Southland,
    Proud heart, be of good cheer,
Thy people's prayers for thee arise,
    Thy life they hold most dear.

We 'll ne'er forget thee while one spot
    Remains where blood was shed,
One memory in our lives is left,
    Of one dear rebel dead.

CARRIER'S NEW YEAR'S ADDRESS.

FOR THE "DALLAS HERALD."

Hushed are the merry Christmas bells,
  The "Old Year," too, has fled
Adown the ways of bygone days,
  Where centuries lie dead.

The "New Year," with her youthful airs,
  Comes forth to take her place ;
Rich wreaths of plenty in her hands,
  And smiles upon her face.

May she her streams of wealth outpour
  Upon her fields and lands ;
Her sunlit smiles upon you fall,
  And bounty from her hands.

Unto our people may she give
  Rare jewels from her breast,
And shelter in her happy arms
  The poor and the oppressed.

Kind friends, the favors freely given
  To us throughout the past,
Once more bestow, they will return,
  Like bread on waters cast.

We labor hard that you may learn,
  Broadcast we drop the leaves ;
Sowing the while that you may reap,
  And garner golden sheaves.

The *Herald* still shall seek to win
  To our young city here,
A goodly name, a wealth of fame,
  To make a prosperous year.

For high and low, for rich and poor ;
  For all, both far and near,
May Time the coming hours entwine
  Into a " Happy Year."

A SERENADE.

Come through the aisles of moss-crowned oaks,
   Down to the banks of the inland sea,
Where the crystal waves in the glimmering light,
   Meet the white shores caressingly.
Where the sand-silvered shells lie row on row,
And the winds in the willows, like sighs, soundeth
      low ;
And the lotus-flowers lift up their snowy-crowned
      heads,
Nodding so lazily o'er their green beds.

Come when the cayman joins in the hum
   Of the insect-world, with his deep bass notes,
And the wild water-fowl, in the darkening day,
   On the crest of the gentle breaker floats.
The glowworm will light a path for thy feet,
And the mocking-bird greet thee lovingly sweet ;
While the breezes will whisper a tale to thee
Of one to be whispered, down by the sea.

Come, rest on the green-crested Indian mound,
   And I 'll tell you how once, in the days of yore,
A dusky maiden, with nimble hand,
   'Broidered a belt with wampum o'er,
For her warrior chief, as she watched the while
For his light canoe, from the low, cypress isle ;
Coming with offerings for her from afar ;
Coming in triumph with trophies of war.

Then my voice will take a tenderer tone,
   As I tell thee a tale of a later day ;
And if the warm blush on thy cheek should burn,
   I 'll kiss it fondly, fair one, away ;
And as the bright stars steal out in the skies,
Fathom my fate in thy dark beaming eyes.
Then haste to the banks of the inland sea,
Where thy true love is sighing and watching for
     thee.

THE LAST VICTORY.

Now waking with the faintest hum,
Is heard the roll of distant drum ;
While answering back from every lea,
Sounds quick, the rebel reveille.

From lowly couches where they lie,
Beneath the arches of the sky,
The slumbering armies wake to life,
And gird them for the coming strife.

Now here, now there, the quivering lights,
Shine out like stars upon the heights ;
While in the distant vales below,
They flit like fireflies to and fro.

See where the Southrons proudly go,
In glittering columns, row on row,
March in unbroken, grand array,
As if 't were some great gala day.

34

But from the strains of fife and drum,
And from the struggle soon to come ;
From scenes of blood and war to-day,
Their thoughts are winging far away

To homes where orange blossoms blow,
Where dark and sluggish bayous flow ;
Where, bounded by sweet summer skies,
All nature dreams and slumbrous lies.

To homes by lakes, upon whose breast
The water-fowl floats at rest ;
And southern lotus-flowers fair,
Their white heads bow as if in prayer.

To homes amid the sighing pines,
That heavenward tower in rigid lines ;
By winding streams, on prairies wide ;
In lowly vales, on mountain side.

Dear ones are there who sadly wait,
The mandates of relentless fate ;
No mirth is there, no sound of song,
Where sadly drag the hours along.

But prayers for those who, far away,
Perchance go down to death to-day ;
Go down with firm, unfaltering tread.
The paths where patriots oft have bled.

They 're marching down the battle plain,
To Dixie's mellow, martial strain ;
While, like an echo from afar,
Come back the foemen's notes of war.

Behold their haughty banner, too,
Its stars engemmed amid the blue ;
Bidding defiance to the world,
In every fluttering fold unfurled.

See, too, the blood-red southern cross,
Amid the flash of bayonets toss ;
The very chargers seem to know
That carnage soon shall reign below.

Hark ! 't is the rebel yell we hear ;
It bears no note, no breath of fear ;
'T is well, they meet no common foe,
But veterans, who 'll give blow for blow.

Who 'll stand like rocks upon the shore
Where tempests have vainly beat before?
The flower of a mighty land,
Undaunted, fearless, firm of hand.

Sons of the sunny land, be bold;
A nation's prayers your hand uphold;
With every breeze that round you blows,
A benediction to you flows.

With eager steps they follow where
Their tattered banners kiss the air;
Like avalanche, they sweep adown,
And charge the heights where batteries frown.

Now mingle in the dreadful fray,
The armies of the blue and gray;
How eyes grow dim, how senses reel,
With flash of arms and clash of steel.

Hark! how the bugle's stirring strain
Calls to them o'er the bloody plain;
The sombre clouds hang dark and low;
Who now can tell a friend from foe?

What deeds of prowess, hand to hand ;
What precious blood dyes all the land ;
And last farewells, breathed out upon
Each field of triumph,—dearly won.

Beside the soldier in his prime,
Lies one just o'er the glad springtime ;
The furrowed cheek, the hoary hair
Of age, in death are mingled there.

The sons of toil, with hard-worn hands,
The lord of slaves and princely lands,
The blood of churl and cavalier,
Now mingle in one common bier.

But evening shadows creep around
The pathways of the battle ground ;
And peace is brooding once more where
Harsh battle thunders rent the air.

The southern cross floats once again
In victory o'er the unnumbered slain ;
In victory, but it is the last ;
The coming tempest lowers fast.

O oft-tried troops, the python coils
Of fate will crush you in its toils !
There is no cloud to go before ;
No rod to span the waters o'er.

What tongue can tell !   Ah ! who can say
The bitter anguish of that day,
When humbled was a haughty race,
And a proud nation veiled her face ?

But let the future, like a pall,
Before those hours of anguish fall ;
Shut out from all the wide world's gaze
The deep despair of those dark days.

Soon will the armies clad in gray
Pass like the mists at dawn of day,
And naught be left but what belongs
To history, and to poet's songs.

TWILIGHT.

FIRST.

'T is a tender, touching time,—
Twilight in a southern clime :
Then the music softly wakes
From the tangle of the brakes.
To and fro the evening breeze
Sways the sombre moss-hung trees,
By the inland lakes that lie,
Softly silvered, 'neath the sky.
On the crystal waves are seen,
Floating up, long arms of green,
To the night dews holding up,
Each a pure-white chalice cup.
Lilies blooming everywhere
Like the wondrous lotus fair.
By the low isles, all unseen,
Swims the cayman in between ;
Soon his bellowings, loud and harsh,
Wake the night birds from the marsh ;
Circling here and there they fly,
Some with hoarse, discordant cry ;

Some with twitterings, soft and low,
Where the sluggish bayous flow.
The forests, skies, the very ground,
Seem filled with one harmonious sound,
'T is nature's vesper o'er the land,
Sent heavenward by an unseen hand.

SECOND.

Ah ! 't is a tender, touching time,—
Twilight in a southern clime :
Then the night with solemn tread,
Advancing, tells us : " Day is dead."
A time to gather to the fold
Of retrospection, thoughts of gold ;
Of resolutions to attain
Those promised robes without a stain.
A time when truths eternal seem
The ladder of the seer's dream,
By which our world-worn spirits rise
Unto the heights of angel skies.
Ah ! when our heavenly day is done,
May heavenly twilight fall upon
Us gently, as this twilight time,
All glorious in a southern clime.

RUTH ALLEN.

Pretty Ruth Allen from morn to eve,
As fast as her slender fingers could weave,
Broidered a banner of silken bars,
And a blue field glittering with silver stars.
In the twilight's beauty, at early dawn,
Pretty Ruth Allen wove on and on,
While her voice trilled out in gladsome rhyme,
A gallant deed of the olden time.

Pretty Ruth Allen from sun to sun,
Labored until the work was done,
Then said : " 'T is a banner for the brave,
And this is the only boon I crave,
That when my own hero shall sink to his rest,
His comrades shall fold it over his breast.
And the stars that enrich it like those up above
Shall burn on his bosom, the stars of my love."

Under the banners of Southern moss,
Ruth Allen sits weaving a Southern cross,

There in the light of the dying day,
Weaving a cross of symbolic gray.
Her cheeks are pale, and her eyes are dim,
And she sings no more, but weeps for him ;
And her heart, now ladened with sorrow and care,
Goes back to that day of death and despair,
When a lover was lost, when a field was won,
And her life-joys went down like a setting sun.

YOUTH AND AGE.

Upon the gleaming heights I stood,
   It seems so long ago,
About me heaven's glories shone,
   The skies were all aglow.
Far, far below the valleys spread,
   Inviting, cool, and green,
The rugged rocks seem golden walls,
   With silvery streams between.

With longing eyes I looked, and cried,
   "O ! shall I never reach,
The valleys with their winding ways,
   The far-off shining beach,
Where murmurs of the mighty tide,
   The music of the waves,
Seem ever like sweet solemn songs,
   Above eternal graves ?"

Ah ! since that time my feet have trod,
   The paths that from above

Lead down from those exalted ways,
  The paths of youth and love.
To-day within the longed for-shade
  I stand, and hear the sea ;
The radiant heights, far off and dim,
  Have lost their majesty.

Tho' oft the darkening shadows creep
  Around me lowering low,
Within my soul there is no fear,
  No longings backward flow.
For voices fond seem calling,
  Methinks I feel the spray
Of waters on my cheek and brow,
  Where I shall float some day.

Borne onward to the distant shore,
  Where burdens are cast down,
And time shall wreathe the thorns no more
  Into the waiting crown.
Eternity ! what heaven-born hopes,
  Shall blossom from despair,
What endless dreams of youth and love,
  Unfold immortal there!

THE DEATH OF STONEWALL JACKSON.

The great rebel chief lay dying,
  Dying, almost dead,
While pressing close around him
  Were the troops he oft had led.
They are true, and tried, and faithful,
  The soldiers gathered there,
But their hearts are sinking now
  With a measureless despair.

O'er the hills of old Virginia,
  By river-side, on plain,
And through her tangled forests,
  Amid her fields of grain,
His fortunes they had followed
  With weary, willing feet ;
He had led them oft to glory,
  But never to defeat.

Now he is marching down to death ;
  They cannot follow there.

He fights the last great fight alone,
  With penitence and prayer.
The icy hand is on his heart,
  His eagle eye grows dim,
While his voice is faint and failing,
  As a distant vesper hymn.

His pale lips faintly murmur :
  " How sweet the evening breeze ;
Let us cross o'er the river,
  And rest beneath the trees."
Perchance he had a vision
  Of some great victory won,
And a rest for his weary warriors
  Now that the work was done.

He died—and on the bosom
  Of the grand old mother State
The Southern soldier slumbers
  Amid the good and great,—
A fitting resting-place for one
  Who died for liberty.
Heaven grant him everlasting bliss
  In the great eternity !

THE IDEAL LAND.

Beyond the boundaries of the real,
   There lies the realm of ideal land ;
And all are sovereigns who enter there,
   Where the gates eternally open stand.

And there where the ages are as a day,
   In their flight over fairy fields,
Fancy a wonderful woof of dreams
   From a mystical distaff reels.

There one may enter, and leave behind,
   As a garment is cast away,
The weary thoughts that oppress the soul,
   And the cares that belong to clay.

O ideal land ! who has not felt
   The magical breezes that fill
The sails of ships on thy endless seas,
   Where the happy ones float at will ?

Who has not walked there, hand in hand,
   'Neath the light of a glorious sun,
With the phantom loves that never have lived,
   And the souls that may never be one ?

'T is a land where the flowers are ever ours,
   Where mortals may sow and reap,
And the sacred treasures we win and wear
   Our souls may in secret keep.

The lonely and sad find a welcome there,
   At home in the palaces grand,
Where tears float away before laughter and love,
   The mists of that ideal land.

O beautiful land, where hearts never grow cold !
   Dear land of the lofty and leal !
Who would not turn to thy limitless life
   From the dreary confines of the real ?

THE UNVEILING OF THE STATUE OF GENERAL A. S. JOHNSON.

Unveil the statue ; let the living here
Look once again upon the form so dear.
   Behold ! a nation's soldier and her pride,
One of those great undaunted souls,
About whose memory her love enfolds,
   And say : " 'T is well he died."

Where shall we find beneath the sky
More fitting spot to raise on high
   A tribute to the brave ?
For here they sleep on every side,
The men who for their country died,
   A hero in each grave.

Unveil the statue ; 't is his place,
A noble son of high-born race,
   To rise above the throng ;
And ours to keep, through coming days,

His fame unsullied, and give praise
  That to his deeds belong.

Thank Heaven, he never knew defeat,
But death to him came swift and sweet,
  And 'round him as he fell,
The strife of battle, like a sea,
Flowed onward in its majesty :
  Soñ of the South ! 't was well.

He perished—'t was a bloody day—
When leading on the columns gray,
  And carnage reigned around ;
His men about him row on row,
Amid the mighty ebb and flow
  Of battle strewed the ground.

Heavenward their valiant souls arose,
And at the evening's solemn close
  His spirit led the van.
The cannons' roar the echoes woke,
The gleam of bayonets thro' the smoke,
  Like silver streamlets ran.

Like breath of tempest o'er the land,
They onward swept, the armies grand,
  As storms where mountains frown,

And floated high the flags of war,
The cross, the crescent, and the star,
　　Where rebel ranks rushed down.

Then darkness let her mantle fall
Above the landscape like a pall
　　Upon each weary breast ;
Where soldiers slumbered, far and wide,
To dead and living side by side,
　　The night had brought sweet rest.

So 'mid the darkness and the dust
Of long gone years where bright swords rust,
　　And battle banners lie,
We 'll lay away our memories sad,
With triumphs that have made us glad,
　　And names that cannot die.

Unveil the statue ; through the years
Let those who tread here shed no tears,
　　Nor feel one throb of pain.
For Patriot's blessings o'er him breathe,
Immortal names with his enwreathe.
　　Who 'll say he died in vain ?

THE VOUDOO.

The voudoo sings her weird witch song,
Adown the brakes, the lakes along ;
She stoops where deadly blossoms blow,
About her feet the fire-flies glow.

The gliding serpent from her path
Turns not, but sounds the note of wrath ;
She heeds it not, but laughs in glee,
And plucks the death blooms from the tree.

Down by the bayous and the banks
Where rushes raise their spear-like ranks,
O'er grass-grown ways, by marshy fens,
Where mosses, massed, enwrap the glens,

She nightly takes her lonely way,
Shunning the brightness of the day,
Waking from out the dewy grasses,
The humming insects where she passes.

The cayman from his slimy bed
Lifts to the lights his horny head,
His bellowings break the night-bird's rest,
And sends it fluttering from its nest.

It hooting waves its goblin wings
Above the voudoo as she sings :
" Awake, O bloom of beauty, wake !
From out thy bosom death I take."

Whene'er I will, fond hearts grow cold,
Breath of my life, thy leaves unfold,
Flowers of vengeance and of hate,
My eager hands above you wait.

She sees the day-star hung on high,
A crystal ball far up the sky,
And wanders back thro' marsh and fen,
Like some fierce beast, to its dark den.

Back to the hut beside the lake,
Behind it lies the sunless brake,
About it gorgeous flowers entwine,
The jessamine and the scarlet vine.

But deadly night-shade grows between,
And serpents coil amid the green ;
There spiders swing their silken beds,
And treacherous reptiles raise their heads.

Within, O dare not, tread not there,
Death breathes upon the very air,
Naught but a creature vile could dwell
One moment in that earth-wrought hell.

A creature lost apart from earth,
A demon smiled upon thy birth,
Accursed in life, in death no friend
Shall o'er thy couch in anguish bend.

Upon thy brow the brand of Cain,
What hand shall soothe thy bitter pain?
Ah ! well, perchance some good is brought
From out the ruin thou hast wrought.

In human lives, a soul but gives
The good or ill that in it lives.
Who can condemn, since God dictates
The destiny his power creates?

DEAD ON THE FIELD OF HONOR.

In a fair land beyond the sea,
Whose banners bear the fleur de lis,
A band of heroes there 't is said,
Answering the roll-call for the dead,
Say for each gallant comrade slain
In battle, on some world-known plain,
" Dead on the field of honor."

And now whene'er brave soldiers meet,
Amid the tramp of martial feet,
The beat of drum, the warlike strain
Of " Dixie Land " heard once again,
The living there may proudly say :
" They sleep, our comrades true to-day,
Upon the field of honor."

Where'er the sweep of wandering winds
Makes music thro' the solemn pines,
Where mountains linked across the land

Enchain the depths of forests grand,
From sea to sea, by rushing river,
They lie, dead—but forgotten never—
Upon the field of honor.

Yes, dead, but in remembrance still
Their glorious names our hearts will thrill.
Sons of the South, their noble deeds,
Upspringing in your hearts as seeds,
Will bid you bear thro' coming wars
The memory of the stars and bars
Upon the field of honor.

No more thro' all the coming years
Will they behold the countless spheres,
Hung from abysmal arches high,
The wondrous watchers of the sky,
Nor feel the south wind soft and low,
Where camp-fires once were wont to glow
Upon the field of honor.

No more they hear the rebel yell
Where battle thunders rose and fell ;
'T is now a welcome and a cheer
To friends, to foemen, far and near ;

And peace, sweet peace, born of despair,
Walks forth, and sheds her radiance fair
Upon lost fields of honor.

Peace to the living and the dead,
Peace, for the bloody years now fled.
A nation proud with armies grand,
United, they about her stand,—
Her bold defenders, who will die
In brotherhood beneath the sky
Upon her fields of honor.

And now the living well may say :
Arise, brave spirits, come to-day !
Behold, where in communion sweet
The soldiers of our country meet,
The men who in the days of yore
Bravely their battle banners bore
Upon the field of honor.

We 'll tell our children how they died,
Strewing the land on every side,
The gallant men who wore the blue,
The sons of the Southland, brave and true ;
Of battles lost and battles won,

Of famous deeds beneath the sun,
Upon the field of honor.

And heart to heart and hand to hand,
When outward foes assail the land,
The world will see these armies vast
Wipe out the hatred of the past.
Behold the valiant and the brave,
Seek then one glory and one grave
Upon the field of honor.

THE BORDER-LAND.

Far out on the frontier they dwell,
A people alone,
Where the breezes make moan
About their rude homes in the forest,
Where the white-veined leaves are never at rest,
And the spider weaves ever its silvery spell,
In the bower where the song-bird buildeth her nest.

The smoke from their hearth-stones to heaven
  ascends
Like the incense of prayer.
No altars are there,
But nature her sermons unfold,
And ever her lessons repeat,
By the murmuring streams and dark woody dells,
Where her voices are mellow and sweet.

Their sons are unlettered and rude,
But true, and as bold

As the heroes of old,
Who have left us their great deeds in story.
Their lives and their loves are enwrought
With no silver threads, and their daily food
By the sweat of their brows is bought.

Their daughters are children of toil and sorrow,
They wear neither jewel nor ring,
But they ofttimes smile, and they sing
While their swift shuttles glance
In and out weaving the homely dyes,
Taking no thought for the cares of to-morrow,
Dreaming naught of the danger that round them
    lies.

They rise and go out in the sunset's gold,
A spirit of rest
Seems the earth to oppress.
The spider has ceased from its spinning ;
The song-bird has hushed its sweet singing ;
The cattle estray have returned to the fold ;
The horn of the hunter through the forest is ring-
    ing.

A rain-cloud ascends and floats out on the sky ;
The darkness descends

O'er the dim wooded lands ;
The moccasined feet of the savage come stealthily
Astir in the spiritless leaves of the path ;
The shuddering night hears the bloodthirsty cry,
Where the red men arise like demons of wrath.

O'er the ashes of homesteads the sunlight falls ;
The wolf to the thicket,
With jaws blood wet,
Is stealing away ; from its eyrie
The vulture drops down on its prey ;
And no ringing horn through the forest calls,—
Dead are the loves of yesterday.

In the halls of the nation, no sorrow reigns there ;
Our rulers make mirth
With the high ones of earth.
There is joy, there is feasting in lordly homes ;
There are sounds of sweet music and sounds of
        song ;
They hear not the wails of death and despair ;
Nor the voices that cry, " Avenge us our wrongs ! "

THE OLD HOMESTEAD.

Come, memory, with thy witching wand,
And from thy treasured store
   Bring distant days,
   Deserted ways,
That I may tread no more.

Restore the fading pictures
Of that sweet sunlit clime,
   Where tropic vine,
   With flowers entwine,
Beneath the fragrant lime.

I view the sunset's glory,
The morning glowing red,
   The violets sweet
   Beneath my feet,
The roses o'er my head.

The sounds of life uprising
Float o'er me as in dreams,

The lowing herds,
The uttered words,
The murmur of the streams.

I see a grand old mansion,
As in the days of yore,
 All pillared white,
 An isle of light,
Uprising by the shore.

Beyond the fields outspreading,
Like some great restless sea,
 The river grand,
 The forest land,
Enwrapped in mystery.

There are the cabins, row on row,
The sinuous paths between,
 On every side
 The workers glide,
Ghost-like upon the scene.

Once more the anvil ringeth
 Where willow hangeth low,—
 Its branches toss'd,
Like goblins lost,
Down by the dark bayou.

Within the shop the dusky forms,
Beneath the flickering light,
  Seem giants grim ;
  An ancient hymn
Wails out into the night.

It soundeth like a dirge of death
From out the open door,
  The sparks arise
  Like fire-flies,
And die upon the floor.

There float sweet strains of music
From out the mansion walls,
  Where ladies fair,
  With stately air,
Sweep through the spacious halls.

And gallant men are gathered there,
I see them ride away ;
  And then the night
  Shuts out the light
Of many a by-gone day.

Within the ruined homestead now
The swallow builds her nest,

And homeward flies,
When down the skies
The sun-god sinks to rest.

So o'er the gulf that lies between
The dead years and to-night,
To that lost home
My thoughts will roam,
As swallows in their flight.

Go, memory, with thy witching wand,
Why bring back hours long fled ?
'T is all in vain.
Ah bitter pain !
Thou canst not wake the dead.

IN MEMORY OF MRS. GEN. CABELL.

In the great city of the dead,
Silent save for the tears we shed
    And the sweet words of prayer,
The day in regal splendor glowing,
The soft spring odors round us flowing,
    We laid her gently there.

The loving wife, the tender mother,
Ah Death ! could'st not thou find another,
    That thou must take the best ?
We left her alone, the heart so true,
Beneath heaven's starlight and its blue,
    Sweet flowers on her breast.

But we knew her spirit with hastening feet
Had gone where lives are made complete,
    Where never enters care ;
And tho' from her accustomed place
We evermore shall miss her face,
    Our hearts will not despair.

For vast and wide is death's domain ;
He throws his earth-encircling chain
  Around us, and we sleep.
Our best-beloved are his prey,
He bears them from our arms away,
  Tho' we our vigils keep.

The ways he takes, to mortal eyes
Seem viewless pathways to the skies ;
  But as in days of old,
Across the blackness of the night
There lies the stair of heavenly light
  That leadeth to the fold.

From out the gloom dear faces bend,
And earthward glad evangels send;
  Adown the aisles of life
Their glorious anthems ofttimes reach,
The auras of our earth-born speech
  Amid the din of strife.

And through the mighty moving throng,
Of mortals comes a solemn song,
  Swift as the wingéd dove,
Bearing, where stormy waters flow

Across the darkness of our woe,
  The olive branch of love.

And then we know some blesséd day,
When earthly visions pass away,
  Awaiting God's behest,
No more o'erwhelmed by wave and wind,
United with our dead we 'll find,
  The mount on which to rest.

THE SONG OF THE SUN.

God of the planets, monarch of day,
    I reign in the realms of space,
And night waves her pinions, and flees away
    From the light of my luminous face.

I drink from the streamlets and seas of earth,
    And my rays on their cold waves glance,
Till the streamlets sparkle and shake with mirth,
    And old ocean seems to dance.

I kiss the fairest flowers that bloom,
    And the fields of waving green,
Shedding a radiance round each tomb,
    Where the steps of decay are seen.

I mark the hours and days that roll
    In the golden circles of years,
And ever on earth new beauties unfold,
    Chasing away gloomy fears.

Weird witches and goblins, and spirits lost
   Turn from my light away,
To the shadows of night and the far distant coast
   Where darkness dwells with dismay.

For music I have the song of the spheres,
   Bright stars that around me shine,
Making melody sweet through endless years,
   Bathed in my light divine.

A monument of immortality,
   Of life in a brighter land,
A type of the soul that will never die,
   Through endless ages I 'll stand.

TO THE BEREAVED.

We lay our children 'neath the sod
   With tears of desolation,
While angels in the treasure-house of God
   Behold their bright translation.

Their precious lives like incense rise
   From the cathedral earth,
Fond mothers' hearts the burning sacrifice,
   Where'er the human race has birth.

Death's ever dark and mystic way
   Is made a path of flowers,
And lightened into glorious day
   By these offerings of ours.

What mother's soul does not arise,
   When these sweet ties are riven,
Unto the heights of spirit skies,
   The lattices of heaven?

What mother fears to follow where
   These little feet have trod,
Unto the radiant kingdom there,
   The garner-house of God?

HUMILITY.

The God of day, low down the sky,
  Hung glittering like a shield,
While round him clouds of every dye
  Gleamed from a golden field,
And as the rays shot up to heaven,
  And showered down their glorious beams,
It seemed as if the earth had risen
  To gild her forests and her streams.

O earth ! I said, how vain thou art,
  To think the light of heaven thine own,
For know thy glory shall depart
  When those bright beams have flown ;
And all thy streamlets and thy fields
  Shall rayless lie upon thy breast,
When night her cheerless sceptre wields
  Above a weary world at rest.

How like to man, the man of sin,
  Who basks beneath the light divine,

And vainly dreams that from within
  His soul the eternal glories shine.
God grant us then the grace to see
  That by His love, the sun,
We 'll shine through all eternity,
  When heavenly heights are won.

THE MISSISSIPPI.

O mighty river, pure and sparkling as a little child !
Thou springest up amid the snow-clad hills,
And cometh down to us thro' tangled brake and
    wild,
With blackened waters grown to manhood and to
    madness ;
Down by the modest hamlet and the crowded city,
Down by the homes of sin and suffering and
    sorrow,
Down by the homes of joy and mirth and revelry.
Thou flowest ever with the self-same fretful mur-
    mur ;
Thou bearest on thy broad black breast
A little world, a nation's wealth ;
And in thy dead cold bosom rests
The golden treasures of full many hearts.
How oft in happy childhood would I stray
Upon the white sands girding in thy shore,
That like a strand of silver lights the way

Thy murky waters murmur to the sea.

How oft have stooped to write in glee

Some name loved, and familiar then ;

Names of the dear ones, who as shadows seem

To dwell in far-off lands, or in sweet dreams.

Ah ! like the peasant from the Alpine heights,

Who glories in the deadly avalanche,

My heart with thoughts of thee will thrill

Until I cross the full dark stream of death.

Father of Waters ! rushing, restless river, on thy
 shore

How many hopes have wrecked,

And homes that late resplendent shone now lie

Deserted and in mouldering ruins ;

Black walls and broken tell of days gone by,

And mark the ways where mighty armies trod.

Upon thy banks were fertile fields, and many a plain

That rivalled famed Cathay,

Crowned with the tasselling corn and emerald cane,

That on the earth like green enamelling lay.

Ceres poured forth her gifts with bounteous hand ;

And from her trailing garments sprung

Bright flowers that carpeted the land

Like those beneath a tropic sun.

But flowers are faded now, and fields lie bare,

Many untrod, untilled by man,
Who turns from scenes so desolate and drear
With clouded brow and tear-dimmed eyes.
O river ! ever running to the sea,
Tell to the sounding depths the sorrows of our
     people ;
Tell how in vain we struggled to be free ;
Tell of our loved ones lost for liberty.
Let them lie there, forever buried, where
The hurricane will sound a lasting dirge,
And wailing winds, in wild despair,
Mourn o'er our downfall and our destiny.

www.ingramcontent.com/pod-product-compliance
Lightning Source LLC
Chambersburg PA
CBHW032357020726
47499CB00008B/2787

* 9 7 8 3 3 3 7 2 7 2 5 5 5 *